D1223350

TALES OF THE TIGRESS

SIMON SPOTLIGHT
An imprint of Simon & Schuster Children's Publishing Division
1230 Avenue of the Americas, New York, New York 10020
This Simon Spotlight edition June 2015
© 2015 Viacom International Inc. All Rights Reserved. NICKELODEON and all related logos are trademarks of Viacom International Inc. Based on the feature film "Kung Fu Panda," © 2008 DreamWorks Animation LLC. All Rights Reserved. All rights reserved, including the right of reproduction in whole or in part in any form. SIMON SPOTLIGHT and colophon are registered trademarks of Simon & Schuster, Inc. For information about special discounts for bulk purchases, please contact Simon & Schuster Special Sales at 1-866-506-1949 or business@simonandschuster.com.
Manufactured in the United States of America 0515 FFG
10 9 8 7 6 5 4 3 2 1
ISBN 978-1-4814-2828-6 (pbk)
ISBN 978-1-4814-2829-3 (hc)
ISBN 978-1-4814-2830-9 (eBook)

TALES OF THE TIGRESS

adapted by Judy Katschke

Simon Spotlight
New York London Toronto Sydney New Delhi

KUNG FU
DAY CARE

CHAPTER **ONE**

Tigress knew how to claw her way to the top.

So after leaping from mountain ledge to ledge, the fearless kung fu warrior began her rock-steady climb.

"Arrgh." Tigress grunted, digging her sharp claws into the mountainside. She knew she wasn't alone because bringing up the rear was the legendary, oozing-with-awesomeness Dragon Warrior Po!

"Can't . . . hold on . . . much . . ." Po gasped, clinging desperately to a crag. He felt himself slip and yelled, "Heeeeeeeeelp!"

Tigress groaned. It didn't take a genius to know that she and Po were as different as yin and yang!

"Po, look down," Tigress said with a sigh.

Po glanced down. His feet were just inches off the ground. Awkward!

"We can eat when we get to the top!" Tigress called.

Eat? Now *that* was the magic word!

Visions of dumplings bounced in Po's head as he scrambled to the top. But instead of finding noodles or stir-fried veggies, Po found a duck!

"Hee-hee!" the little duckling laughed as he

scurried by. Chasing him was a gang of crocodiles!

Po and Tigress could tell who the leader of the gang was. It was the dude with the 'tude, and his name was Fung.

"We got you!" Fung said as they backed the duckling named Zan against a wall.

"Nuh-uh!" Zan said.

"Yuh-uh!" Fung argued when—

"NUH-UH!" Tigress called.

Fung turned. His jaw dropped when he saw Tigress and Po. The warriors had his Croc Bandits in a choke hold!

"Do you know these guys?" Po asked Zan.

"Sure!" Zan said. "They're holding me for ransom!"

Ransom? Po and Tigress struck fighting stances.

Ransom meant one thing: Zan was being duck-napped!

The idea made Po fume. He and the Furious Five had a special job: to protect the Valley

of Peace from evil. And right now evil meant crocodiles!

"Hi-yaaaa!" Tigress shouted, surprising Fung with a lightning-fast side kick. The blow made him drop Zan.

"Wheeeeeee!" Zan laughed as he ran away.

The bandits weren't laughing as they closed in on Tigress and Po. In a flash everybody was kung fu fighting.

Tigress took on three Crocs while Po struck, chopped, and kicked Fung. When that didn't work, Po turned to an ancient kung fu panda technique: the flying wedgie!

Grabbing Fung's pants, Po gave them a stretch. He then let go with a *snap*!

"Ahhhhh!" Fung yelled as he went flying.

Fung and the bandits ran straight for the swamps. Zan ran to Tigress.

"I'm Zan!" he said. "I like you!"

"No, you don't!" Tigress said. She wasn't a fan of kids. And unless it was a kung fu death grip, she didn't do hugs, either.

"I'm Po, and this is Tigress," Po told Zan with a big smile. "Are you sure it isn't *me* you like?"

Zan was totally sure. Tigress was his new bestie. If only Tigress felt the same way about Zan.

CHAPTER **TWO**

Master Shifu sat cross-legged in the Jade Palace, putting out candles one by one. It was a peaceful task. But that day the palace was anything but peaceful. . . .

"Hee-hee!" Zan giggled as he scooted by.

Shifu put out one more candle before bringing Zan to a stop. "Can you tell us where you live?" he asked.

"In the blue house by the big rock." Zan giggled. "Maybe green."

"Thanks for clearing that up," Monkey muttered. Shifu turned to Crane and Viper and said, "I want you to search high and low for Zan's parents."

"Dibs on high!" Crane said, spreading his wings.

"I always get stuck with low," Viper said, sighing.

Tigress wished she could join Viper and Crane— anything to escape Zan!

"What's your favorite color?" Zan said, hugging Tigress' legs.

"Mine is orange with black stripes!"

"Zan has taken a shine to you, Tigress," Shifu said with a smile. "You can look after him."

"What?" Tigress gasped. What was Master Shifu thinking? Everyone in the palace knew she didn't like kids!

Shifu tried to make Tigress understand.

"Zan is in a strange place," he explained. "You know how frightening that can be."

Tigress' eyes grew wide as she remembered. A long time ago she was a small cub in a strange place called the Jade Palace. And she had been frightened too.

"You will take care of Zan," Shifu told Tigress. "And you will at least pretend to be happy about it."

"Yes, Master Shifu." Tigress sighed.

"Yay!" Zan cheered.

Po promised to keep an eye on Tigress. She had no experience with kids, but he did. He even knew how kids thought!

"Because you've got the mind of a child," Monkey pointed out.

"Exactly!" Po said proudly.

Later, when Po looked for Tigress, he found her in the kung fu training room. Instead of playing with Zan, she was fighting off swinging spiked pendulums, and crushing wheels.

"Are you checking up on me?" Tigress demanded.

"Yeah . . . sort of," Po admitted.

But where was Zan?

Po screamed as a giggly Zan swung by—tied to a spiky ball!

Quickly, Po untied Zan. He knew Tigress wasn't exactly babysitter of the year. But did she

have to be so cranky and clueless about kids?

"Kids need hugs and stuff," Po told Tigress. "You didn't get a lot of hugs when you were a kid, did you?"

"Hugs are for the weak!" Tigress snapped. "I nestled in the warm embrace of kung fu training."

Po's eyes lit up. Kung fu—that's it!

"Why don't you embrace Zan in some training?" Po suggested.

"Fine," Tigress said.

Zan was itching to give kung fu a try. But each time he kicked, he fell back on his tail.

"He's hopeless!" Tigress groaned.

Po told Tigress to have patience. Kung fu was all about patience—but to Zan it was about *fun*.

"I like kung fu!" Zan squealed. He grabbed a huge spiky wheel and spun it right into Tigress!

"Oof!" Tigress grunted. Fighting hordes of evil villains was more fun than babysitting. And a lot easier!

That night, Tigress tucked Zan into bed. She said good night as she left the room.

"Good night, Mama," Zan said sleepily.

Tigress froze. Whoa—she never signed up for that!

But after Tigress closed the door, Zan had another nighttime visitor. It wasn't the tooth fairy. Or the sandman. It was one of the Furious Five's worst nightmares—Fung!

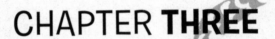

CHAPTER **THREE**

"He's right in here," Fung whispered as the bandits broke into Zan's room.

Fung leaned over Zan's bed. "Hey, there, Zanny," he whispered. "How are you doing?"

"Sleepy, Mr. Crocky-dile," Zan mumbled.

Fung's sidekick, Gah-ri, watched as Fung picked up Zan. "Are we going to leave a ransom note?" he asked eagerly.

"How much are you asking for him?" a voice called out.

"A lot!" Fung chuckled—until he saw Po and Tigress!

"All right, Fung," Po growled.

"Shh!" Fung hissed. "Don't wake him."

"Oh, sorry!" Po whispered too. "It's time to feel the thunder!"

"We brought some thunder of our own!" Fung whispered back.

The bandits held up bamboo poles. Po and Tigress whispered battle cries as they blocked the swinging sticks. They snatched the poles from the Crocs and then used them to pummel their big scaly heads!

"Shakabooey!" Po whispered with one last jab.

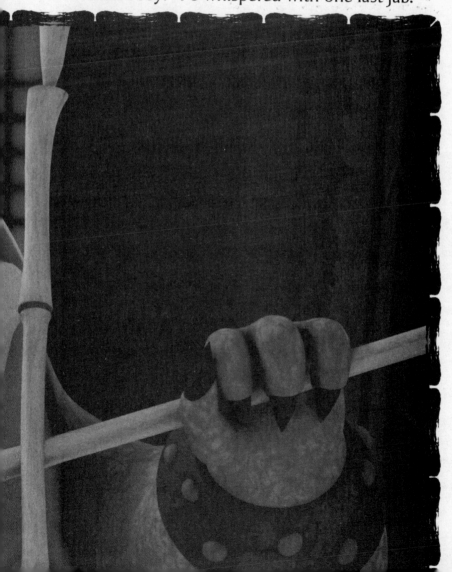

Fung and the bandits retreated out the window, leaving Zan in the bed, dreaming peacefully.

As soon as the battered and bruised Crocs got home, they began dreaming too—dreaming up a new plan!

"Maybe we're no good at this," Gah-ri mumbled.

Fung sighed. Gah-ri had a point. They couldn't even handle a four-year-old kid!

"You're right," Fung said. "We don't have a chance against the Furious Five."

"FUNG!" Fung's mom shouted. "Can your cousin Lidong play with you and your friends?"

"Mom!" Fung shouted back. "Please! I'm not a babysitter—"

CRASH!

A gargantuan crocodile smashed through the door. His head was the size of a pagoda, and his snout was as long as a dragon boat!

"Lidong . . . you grew up," Fung said with a big gulp.

"Whatever we're doing, I get fifty percent of the take," Lidong boomed.

Fung accepted the deal. Fifty percent was a small price to pay for a secret weapon.

Meanwhile, back at the Jade Palace, Shifu had a new task for the Furious Five. . . .

"A farm on the far end of the valley is being

threatened by bandits," Shifu reported. "We have to go help them at once."

"Let's go!" Tigress declared.

Shifu shook his head. "Zan needs a capable protector," he explained. "And that's you."

While Shifu, Po, Monkey, and Mantis set off, Tigress stayed behind. She went back to teaching kung fu to Zan.

"I'm sorry, Tigress," Zan said after accidentally kicking Tigress in the chin.

Tigress couldn't believe a kid could hit so hard—until she remembered herself when she was learning kung fu. She was a hard hitter but a clumsy kicker. Shifu taught her the value of patience. And Tigress remembered he taught her something else. . . .

"Hey, Zan," Tigress said, smiling. "Do you know how to play checkers?"

Soon, Tigress and Zan sat over a checkerboard and a game was in progress. But just as Tigress was about to make the next move—

SMASH!

A massive crocodile's foot came down on the board. Tigress looked up . . . and up . . . and gasped. Looming over her was the biggest, meanest-looking crocodile ever!

"Fung was right!" Lidong yukked. "This is going to be FUN!"

CHAPTER **FOUR**

"There's the farmhouse!" Po said, pointing.
A woman screamed inside the house. Someone was in trouble!

Po, Monkey, Mantis, and Shifu stormed the farmhouse. But instead of finding a woman in trouble, they found one of Fung's bandits disguised in a wig. It was a setup!

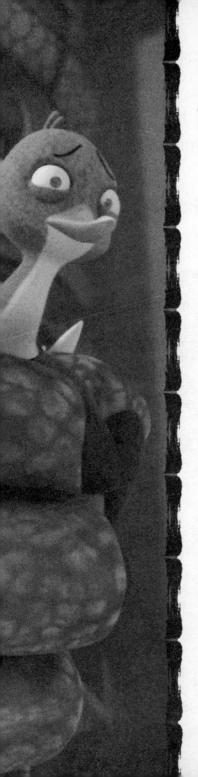

"Fung is snatching that kid," another bandit blurted. "And there's nothing you can do about it."

After a furious kung fu battle, the warriors defeated the bandits and were on their way back home.

"We've got to get back to the palace!" Po said.

Meanwhile, back at the Jade Palace, Fung had grabbed Zan.

"I've got the kid—let's go!" Fung told Lidong.

Tigress kicked and clawed. Her skills were no match for the strength and size of Lidong—until she swung both feet in the air, giving Lidong a powerful flying kick that sent him reeling!

Lidong came back fighting. He clawed at Tigress, but she ducked every swipe. Fuming, Lidong thrust Tigress against a wall.

As Lidong held Tigress, he shouted to Fung, "Get the kid out of here!"

Tigress had to think fast. Spotting a ball on the ground, she kicked it against the wall. It bounced hard, hitting Lidong square in the head!

"Owwww!" Lidong howled. His claws reached up to rub his head. Tigress was free!

Fung and Gah-ri raced down the stairs, Tigress at their heels. But before Tigress could grab Zan

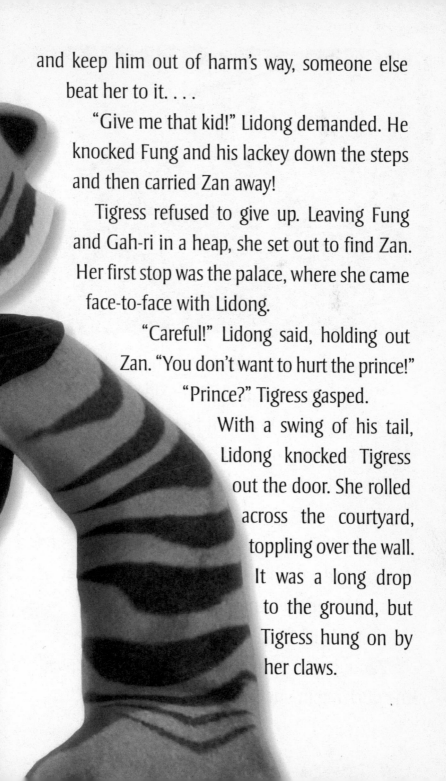

and keep him out of harm's way, someone else beat her to it. . . .

"Give me that kid!" Lidong demanded. He knocked Fung and his lackey down the steps and then carried Zan away!

Tigress refused to give up. Leaving Fung and Gah-ri in a heap, she set out to find Zan. Her first stop was the palace, where she came face-to-face with Lidong.

"Careful!" Lidong said, holding out Zan. "You don't want to hurt the prince!"

"Prince?" Tigress gasped.

With a swing of his tail, Lidong knocked Tigress out the door. She rolled across the courtyard, toppling over the wall. It was a long drop to the ground, but Tigress hung on by her claws.

"Any last words?" Lidong sneered.

"Yes!" Tigress shouted. "Zan! Side kick!"

Zan gave Lidong a swift kick in the snout. The kick did nothing but make Lidong mad!

"I'm going to . . ." Lidong growled.

"You're not going to do anything to him!" Tigress yelled. She pulled herself up, surprising Lidong with a rapid front kick. Zan flew out of Lidong's hand and onto the ground.

"Run, Zan!" Tigress shouted.

Zan ran, but he didn't get far. Lidong grabbed the duckling in one swipe.

"Let him go!" Tigress demanded.

Fueled by rage, Tigress attacked Lidong with rapid front punches and heel kicks. The crocodile bully tumbled over the wall backward, grabbing the edge with one claw. His other claw gripped Zan!

"If I'm not getting him," Lidong said, "no one is!"

Tigress glared at Lidong. Then through gritted teeth she said, "Nobody . . . hurts . . . my . . . Zan!"

Tigress grabbed Lidong's snout. She lifted him high, swinging him until he dropped Zan. As Tigress snatched Zan, Lidong went flying through the air and over the wall!

"Ahhhhhhhhhh!"

Lidong's screams trailed off as he dropped

hundreds of feet to the forest below. Zan was safe.

Tigress hugged Zan tight.

"I'm never letting you out of my sight again!" Tigress said. As she continued to hug Zan, Crane and Viper appeared.

"We've got company!" Crane said.

"It's Zan's mother!" Viper said.

"What?" Tigress said. Her heart sank.

It wasn't long before the masters of the Jade Palace stood on the steps, ready to greet Princess Zhu Chunhua.

"Mama!" Zan cried happily.

"Zanny!" Princess Zhu Chunhua exclaimed as her son raced into her open wings. After the two hugged, Zan turned to Tigress.

"Tigress?" Zan asked. "Can you come with us?"

Tigress wanted to go with Zan, but she knew his place was with his mom. And Tigress' place was at the Jade Palace.

"No, Zan," Tigress said gently. "But I promise I'll come visit you."

Zan waved good-bye as he and his mom walked away.

"Master Shifu," Tigress said. "I want to thank you."

"For what?" Master Shifu asked.

"For teaching me how to play checkers!" Tigress said with a smile.

Po smiled too. Tigress had found her inner cub. She had also found an awesome new friend: a duckling by the name of Zan.

A TIGRESS TALE

CHAPTER **ONE**

The sun rose over the Jade Palace as Tigress jumped out of bed. She took a deep breath and then centered herself by using her favorite Tai Chi poses.

The skilled kung fu warrior was all set to start another day of doing what she did best: protecting the Valley of Peace from evil. But first it was time for breakfast. . . .

Tigress left her room and padded down the hall. She stopped when she heard Po's voice.

"I see yooooooou!"

Who was Po talking to? Tigress stepped into Po's room and then sighed. Po was talking in his sleep and having another sweet dream!

"I see you, Mr. Cookie." Po giggled. "There's no evading my mouth of fury! Yummy, yummy!"

Tigress rolled her eyes. Po's head was filled with food, even in his sleep.

As usual, Tigress was the first to arrive for breakfast. And, as always, her breakfast was three small tofu squares.

"Gooooooooood mooooooorning!" Po shouted, plopping down next to Tigress. He was wide-awake now as he frowned down at Tigress' bowl. "Ew! I don't know how you can eat that!"

Tigress tried to ignore Po, but it wasn't easy!

"I like bean buns in the morning," Po said, pointing to his own bowl. "It's the perfect break-fast food."

In a flash they were joined by the other four members of the Furious Five—Viper, Crane,

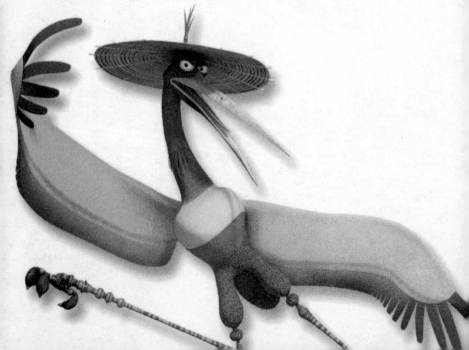

Monkey, and Mantis. They all started talking about food.

"Ooo, bean buns!" Crane cried.

"Yummy!" Mantis and Monkey piped in.

Everyone crowded around Po's bowl, talking at once. Tigress' claw tightened around her chopsticks. Where in the Valley of Peace could a tiger *eat* in peace?

Just then someone cried from outside: "Emergency! Emergency! They're almost here!"

Po and the Furious Five knew that voice anywhere. It was the goose Zeng, and he was in trouble.

"Zeng, what is it?" Tigress asked as they met

him in the courtyard. But Zeng was so choked up, he couldn't speak another word.

"My dad's a goose, I'll handle this," Po said calmly. He stretched his arms and cracked his knuckles, and then he turned to Feng and shouted, "WHAAAAAAT?"

"What's going on here?" Master Shifu asked as he stepped outside.

Zeng pointed a shaking wing at the steps. Someone was approaching the palace. "Mugan!" he cried.

"Mistress Mugan?" Master Shifu gasped. His eyes popped wide open.

"Who's Mistress Mugan?" Po asked.

The Furious Five explained as they hurriedly cleared the courtyard of training apparatuses.

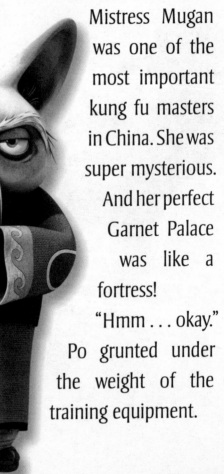

Mistress Mugan was one of the most important kung fu masters in China. She was super mysterious. And her perfect Garnet Palace was like a fortress!

"Hmm . . . okay." Po grunted under the weight of the training equipment.

The masters of the Jade Palace stood at attention. A platform draped with a fancy silk curtain was carried up the steps by a team of goat attendants.

The first attendant, Wu Yong, stepped forward. "Mistress Mugan!" he announced.

The curtain was drawn. A cascade of bubbles fluttered before their eyes. Po and the Furious Five gasped. "Whoaaaa! Check it out!"

Underneath the curtain was a water-filled tank.

Glaring out with piercing jade-green eyes was . . .
a fish!

"Are you serious?" Po laughed.

Mistress Mugan was *very* serious.

"We must talk now!" she told Master Shifu. "In
private."

Po didn't get it. Why was Mugan at the Jade Palace? And what did she want with Master Shifu? Something about this was definitely fishy.

CHAPTER **TWO**

Po and the Furious Five waited while the kung fu masters spoke behind closed doors. A stony-faced attendant stood at attention, guarding the door.

"Hey, buddy," Po told the attendant. "Know what's going on in there?"

The guard stood stiff as a nunchaku, staring straight ahead.

At last the door flew open and Master Shifu stepped out. Behind him was Mugan, who didn't waste time. She got right to the point. . . .

"My top warrior is no longer able to fulfill his duties," Mugan said. "I'm here seeking his replacement."

Mugan glared at the Furious Five. "Shifu has graciously agreed to let me offer the position to one of you five," she said.

Po did the math. Hey, wait! There were six of them—including him!

"If you think one of us six is going to leave the Jade Palace—" Po started to say.

"I wasn't talking to you, panda!" Mugan cut in. "I'm talking to *real* warriors who didn't bungle their way to the top!"

"Did she just insult me?" Po whispered.

"Yeah," Monkey whispered back.

Mugan then warned the Furious Five that the Garnet Palace was a place of absolute order and dedication to kung fu.

"You will have until this evening to give an answer!" Mugan snapped.

Po smirked. As if that was going to happen!

At dinner, Po, Monkey, Crane, Viper, and Mantis yukked it up over their noodles.

"Who does Mistress Mugan think she is?" Po laughed. "Who'd want to leave the Jade Palace and live with her?"

"Me!" Tigress blurted.

What? Po turned to stare at Tigress. She had to be kidding, right? Wrong!

"I've already talked with Mistress Mugan," Tigress explained. "I'm going with her. We leave tonight."

Tigress' words hit Po like a ton of wet wontons. Tigress? Leave? No way!

"But you belong at the Jade Palace," Po insisted. "It's your home, and you love it here!"

"Not anymore," Tigress said.

"Since when?" Po demanded.

"Since *you* arrived!" Tigress snapped. "Before you came, we didn't talk about food all the time. We took kung fu seriously!"

"I take kung fu seriously," Po insisted.

Tigress rolled her eyes and said, "You spent all of yesterday's training showing Monkey how to make fart noises with his armpit!"

Po begged Tigress to stay. He promised to change, but it was no use.

"I don't belong here anymore," Tigress said.

It wasn't long before Tigress was standing at the palace gate with her silk bag packed. Master Shifu, Po, and the Furious Five Minus One came to say good-bye.

"Tigress, are you sure this is what you want?" Shifu asked. He didn't want Tigress to go either, but he knew she had to follow her own path.

"Yes, Master," Tigress replied softly. She then walked over to Mugan's tank.

"Once we leave, you become a warrior of the Garnet Palace," Mugan said. "There is no coming back."

"I understand," Tigress said.

As Tigress followed the procession down the steps, she glanced back. The masters of the Jade Palace looked sad to see her go.

But the saddest face belonged to Po.

CHAPTER **THREE**

"It's been a long journey," Mugan told Tigress as they approached the Garnet Palace. "Rest. You'll need your strength for tomorrow's training."

Tigress didn't want to rest. She wanted to show off her kung fu skills. "I'm ready to begin now!" she declared.

Leaping high, Tigress spun around and around in the air. The second her paws touched the ground, she turned her strength on an army of iron training beasts, smashing them with expert strikes and kicks. She was amazing.

"Hi-yaa!" Tigress shouted when she was done. She smiled at Mistress Mugan.

Was she a kung fu superstar or what?

"You're very powerful," Mugan agreed. Then she scowled and said, "But you lack precision. Let's see how you do against an opponent."

"Who?" Tigress asked.

"Me!" Mistress Mugan replied.

Tigress chuckled to herself. She had heard of the Dragon Form, Snake Form, and Leopard Form, but the Fish Form? Seriously?

"With respect, Mistress," Tigress said. "I—"

WHOOSH!

Mugan shot up out of the tank. She rocketed straight to Tigress, whacking her head with a string of tail slaps. The ferocious fish then switched directions and shot toward a row of water-filled urns!

Tigress watched as Mugan splashed from urn to urn. After refueling, Mugan zoomed back to Tigress, slitting her jacket with razor-sharp fins.

"That was amazing!" Tigress gasped when Mugan was back in her tank.

"That was *precision*!" Mugan said.

Tigress was ready to rest in her new bare-bones room. She sat on her small cot and unpacked. She was surprised to see wooden statues of Po, Monkey, Crane, Viper, and Mantis spill out of her bag onto the bed—so did a note. . . .

"'So you'll never forget us,'" Tigress read aloud. "'Love, Po.'"

Tigress threw the statues and note under the bed. She had no time for play. It was time for serious kung fu training. That meant no dolls, no distractions, and *no Po*!

Back at the Jade Palace, Po had a statue too—of Tigress.

"The Jade Palace is your home!" Po told the doll. "You've got to come back!"

The next morning, Tigress began her first day of training. She hung from a pole and did a hundred gut-crunching pull-ups. She gritted her teeth while balancing rice bowls on her head, shoulders, and knees. She struck the iron beasts so hard, their heads spun around and around!

When she was done, Tigress turned to Mugan. How was that for precision? But the finicky fish shook her head.

The next morning, Tigress tried again. She balanced bigger and heavier rice bowls on her head, shoulders, and knees. She chopped boards in half with her claw. She balanced crushing weights across her shoulders.

Mugan still wasn't sold. It was back to the chopping board for Tigress. Again!

Tigress' stripes were in a twist. What did it take to please the great Mistress Mugan?

Wu Yong was one of Mugan's guards. Tigress had a question for him.

"Wu Yong?" Tigress asked the next morning before training. "What happened to Mistress Mugan's last warrior?"

"He failed her." Wu Yong sighed. "He trained day and night, but no matter how hard he tried, Mugan was never satisfied."

Never satisfied? Tigress' eyes popped wide open. That sounded familiar!

"Year after year he tried to improve," Wu Yong said, "until at last his body began to fail him. He had lived his whole life for kung fu. Without it, he has nothing else. . . . He is broken."

Tigress gulped. Was that *her* fate? Would Mistress Mugan break her body and spirit too? But as she stared at the old goat's sad face, it suddenly clicked. . . .

"It's *you*!" Tigress gasped. "You were the last warrior!"

Suddenly, Mugan appeared at Tigress' door. "What's taking so long?" she demanded as Wu Yong scurried out.

This time Tigress turned to her *inner* strength. Holding her head high, she said, "Mistress Mugan, I think I've made a terrible mistake. I'm afraid I must return to the Jade Palace."

A smile spread across Mugan's face. "I understand completely," she said.

"Thank you!" Tigress said, but then the door shut with a *BANG!*

"You belong to me now!" Mugan told Tigress through a small window on the door. "And like the others before you, I will break you!"

Tigress pushed and pounded, but the bolted door stayed shut. She wouldn't be going back to the Jade Palace anytime soon. In fact, she wouldn't be going anywhere. Tigress was *trapped*!

CHAPTER **FOUR**

Po knocked on the door of the Garnet Palace. He didn't know Tigress was in danger, only that she had to come home!

"I want to see Tigress," Po insisted as Mugan's face appeared at the door.

"She wants nothing to do with you!" Mugan snapped. "Now leave!"

Mugan left an attendant to guard the door. Po surprised him with a swift power punch and then slipped inside. He called Tigress' name as he quickly rushed through the palace.

"In here, Po!" Tigress called back. "Down the hall!"

Po followed Tigress' voice to a door. He could see her eyes through the small window.

"I know you said I don't take kung fu seriously," Po said, "but I'm going to change!"

"Po—" Tigress started to say.

"The Jade Palace is as much your home as it is mine," Po cut in. "And . . . can you open the door, so we can discuss it?"

"I can't!" Tigress said. "I'm locked in. Get me out of here!"

It was Po to the rescue as he charged the door, smashing it down with his shoulder. Tigress was free!

"Don't you dare change!" Tigress told Po with a playful punch. "Now let's get out of here!"

Po and Tigress made their way out of the palace and through the courtyard. Halfway through, they were stopped by a furious Mugan!

"This is your home!" Mugan told Tigress. "You were born to train with me and devote yourself totally to kung fu!"

Tigress remembered Wu Yong's story. "There's more to life than kung fu!" she said.

"Like what?" Mugan shouted.

"Like this!" Tigress stuck her paw under her armpit and then squeaked out a pretty awesome fart noise!

"Nice!" Po laughed. Until . . .

WHOOSH! Mugan shot up out of the tank. She tail slapped Tigress and Po and then zoomed to the urns to power up.

Po watched Mugan splash into the urns, one by one. So that was the secret to her power! Without those urns, the great Mistress Mugan was just another fish out of water!

"That's it!" Po declared.

The stone urns were heavy, but so was Po. He smashed them to the ground, one by one. In a panic, Mugan splashed into the nearest fountain. Grabbing a heavy stone slab, Po covered the fountain—and Mugan. Who was trapped now?

"You're not going anywhere!" Mugan shouted at Tigress through the glass. "You're mine!"

But Tigress didn't belong to anyone but herself!

"You know what, Mistress?" Tigress said coolly. "You really need to lighten up!"

"Thank you," Wu Yong whispered to Tigress and Po. "She's a real . . . meanie."

Side by side, Tigress and Po walked away from the sputtering Mugan. It was time to go back to the Jade Palace. It was time to go *home*!

"So . . . do you want to learn how to burp-talk?" Po asked.

"I don't think so," Tigress said with a smile.

Po smiled too. From this moment on, things would be awesome again. And Tigress was right—there *were* other things in life besides kung fu. Like bean buns . . . and noodles . . . and spring rolls!

And great friends.